The Vikings Have a Field Day

Helaine Becker

Illustrated by
Sampar

Scholastic Canada Ltd.
Toronto New York London Auckland Sydney
Mexico City New Delhi Hong Kong Buenos Aires

Scholastic Canada Ltd.
604 King Street West, Toronto, Ontario M5V 1E1, Canada

Scholastic Inc.
557 Broadway, New York, NY 10012, USA

Scholastic Australia Pty Limited
PO Box 579, Gosford, NSW 2250, Australia

Scholastic New Zealand Limited
Private Bag 94407, Greenmount, Auckland, New Zealand

Scholastic Children's Books
Euston House, 24 Eversholt Street, London NW1 1DB, UK

Library and Archives Canada Cataloguing in Publication
Becker, Helaine, 1961-
The Vikings have a field day / Helaine Becker ; illustrated by Sampar.
(Looney Bay All-Stars ; 3)
ISBN-13: 978-0-439-94623-0
ISBN-10: 0-439-94623-9
1. Vikings–Juvenile fiction. I. Sampar II. Title.
III. Series: Becker
Helaine, 1961- . Looney Bay All-Stars ; 3.
PS8553.E295532V53 2007   jC813'.6   C2006-905224-7

6 5 4 3 2 1   Printed in Canada   07 08 09 10 11

Contents

Chapter 1

Reese McSkittles shivered as he watched the cold grey sea heave and swirl. A thousand years ago Vikings had crossed these same waters. They had landed where Reese was standing now. He hoped it wouldn't happen again.

"Check it out!" a voice called. Reese turned and saw Randall Wetherbury perched on a boulder, pretending to wave a sword. "I'm Leif Ericsson, coolest conqueror of Vinland!"

"You're Randall Wetherbury, looniest loon of Looney Bay," teased Shannon Weiss, nudging him off the boulder. "But you know what *is* cool? This place. It's awesome."

Reese and his friends from Looney Bay Elementary were on a class trip to L'Anse aux Meadows. The Vikings had built the first European settlement in North America here more than a thousand years ago. Now a reconstructed Viking camp stood on the site.

"Aw, it's just some dumb old sod houses," Reese said. He kicked a stone into the surf.

"You're not worried about real-life Vikings showing up here, are you, Reese?" asked Shannon.

Reese wouldn't admit it, but of course he was. People from the past kept appearing from out of nowhere when he was around. Last winter he'd been captured by pirates. Then he'd run into a pair of feuding knights. Somehow hanging around a Viking settlement didn't seem like such a great idea.

"Who, me?" he lied. "Worry about a bunch of Norse nitwits? Nah, we Looney Bay All-Stars can handle a few Berserkers, no problem."

"Yeah, 'cause we're pretty crazy berserk ourselves," said Randall. "Watch this!" He took a run and performed a tremendous long jump. He landed next to Reese.

"Good to see you're back to normal," Randall said. "You were in a bad mood the whole way here. Not the best way to build morale on your track and field team, Captain. The meet against the Marauders is just next week!"

"Maybe he felt seat-sick," said Shannon. She playfully poked Reese in the ribs then ran out of reach. "It's the 100-metre dash! Try and catch me!"

Both Randall and Reese took off after her, whooping and hollering like Viking warriors.

They made it to the visitor centre just as their tour was starting.

As they walked down the slope to the reconstructed Viking site, Reese took his lucky coin from his pocket. He

remembered how he had found it at the hockey rink one day. Actually, it was the same day he'd been captured by the pirates. A while later he'd brought the coin along on a field trip to the Museum of the Middle Ages. He had hoped that a history expert would know more about it. But then the knights had shown up and he'd had to deal with them. Now he wondered if a historian at L'Anse aux Meadows would know its origins.

The coin was gold, but not shiny. There was a design of a lion on one side and a unicorn on the other . . . *or was there?*

Reese peered at the coin. He turned it over in his hand, examining it. There was no unicorn. There was no lion. Instead there were strange letters on

one side, and a picture of a battle-axe on the other.

That's weird, thought Reese. *I was sure it had a unicorn and a lion...*

His steps slowed as he wondered about the coin. Was he remembering it wrong, or had it actually changed? And if it had changed, then why? And how?

He stared at the coin and thought hard. More than ever before, he questioned where it had come from. He looked up to talk to Randall and realized he was standing alone. The group had gone on without him.

"Oh, no," Reese said. "I let them get away from me."

A rope fell around his neck.

A voice hissed in his ear, "They may have got away from you, Skraeling. But you will not get away from me."

Chapter 2

"Let me go!" squawked Reese. The rope was tight around his neck. He looked at his captor. It was just as he'd feared. A tall, powerful Viking was holding the other end of the rope. He was dragging Reese toward a ship.

"I don't think so, my warrior friend," said the Viking.

"I'm not a warrior," Reese replied.

"I'm just a kid."

"Bah!" said the Viking. "I know you Skraelings are small. But you are also fierce, like the giants who dwell in Valhalla, *ja?*"

"I don't even know what Skraelings are!" said Reese. "Honest!"

The Viking stopped short. He faced Reese and examined him closely. "If you are not a Skraeling, then what are you?"

Reese babbled when he was nervous. "I'm a boy, a Newfoundlander and a Canadian. I live down the coast in Looney Bay. I'm captain of the Looney Bay All-Star track team, and our school's best high-jumper . . ."

"Huh," grunted the Viking. "Perhaps you tell the truth. I must be careful: the Skraelings are the mortal enemies of my people. They bedevil us throughout these waters. Do you know the people of which I speak?"

"Never heard of them. I bet they heard the Vikings were back and decided to leave," said Reese. "Speaking of leaving, I'd better be on my way . . ." He tried to yank the rope from the Viking's fist.

But the Viking held the rope and grinned. "I like you, boy. You have the spirit of Loki, the trickster god. What is your name?"

"Reese McSkittles. Who are you?"

"Leif Ericsson."

Reese's eyes nearly bugged out of his head. "You're Leif Ericsson? *The* Leif Ericsson?"

"So my name is known even

amongst the tribe of Looney Bay? That pleases me indeed. Come, you must tell me more of your people. You will be my guest, and we will feast to you tonight, *ja?* You cannot refuse Viking hospitality." There was more warning than welcome in Leif's voice.

Reese gulped hard. Even though he wasn't the least bit hungry, he decided to accept the invitation.

"My men will return soon," Leif said as they boarded the ship. "They are hunting so we can provision the long-house and begin our season here. We will fish and collect timber — and grapes. They love grapes back home."

"Um, Leif," said Reese. "Grapes haven't grown around here for about a zillion years."

"You obviously don't know this land as I do," Leif said. "Why just last year we returned with such a cargo of dried grapes that it brought joy to the people of Greenland for the entire year."

Reese sighed. He hated having to tell his time-travelling visitors the truth — that they'd been mysteriously spirited from their own lives into the future.

That everything they knew was gone. And the world was different — very different.

Leif took it better than most. He cried like a baby for about fifteen minutes. Then he wiped his eyes on his linen shift and brushed his blond hair from his face.

"No grapes?" he sniffled.

"No."

"No timber?" he whimpered.

"There's lots of lichen," said Reese.

Suddenly, Leif's face brightened.

"No Skraelings, either?" he asked, his voice quavering with hope.

"Not a one," said Reese.

Leif leapt to his feet and bellowed, "Then this land is mine! Mine, mine, mine, all mine!"

"Not exactly," Reese said.

"Why not?" Leif asked, bristling. "My longhouses are here, *ja?* As is my forge. I found this land, I claimed this land and I am here today on this land. It is mine."

"Tell that to the Canadian government," Reese said. "They're the ones who rebuilt the place."

"What is this word, 'Canadian'? It is the second time you have said it." Leif's eyes narrowed. "You called yourself a Canadian, I recall. Are you one of the *Canadians* who claim this land?" Leif demanded.

"No. I mean, yes, but . . . Come on, Leif! I'm just a kid!"

"Then you will make a good hostage until I find someone to challenge for this land. I will not give it up without a fight." Leif grabbed Reese and tied him to the mast.

"What about the feast? What about 'Viking hospitality?'" Reese complained.

"Rest assured, boy, there will be a feast. When Vinland is mine. Whether you will be alive to share in it, only time will tell."

Chapter 3

Reese was still tied up when Leif's crew returned. He counted thirty-four men. All of them smelled.

Leif called a council. The Vikings gathered round to hear what he had to say. He went on and on. Reese's favourite part went like this: "the hostage will not be harmed."

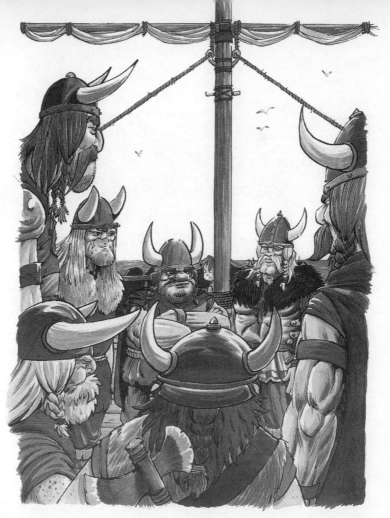

Thorvald, who had two rotten teeth and a nose shaped like a Swedish meatball, said, "Aw, Leif! Can we not use him to sharpen our battle-axes?"

Ingmar, the Viking with a head shaped

like a Danish, said, "Or to practise our knife-throwing aim?"

"No!" replied Leif. "It is nearing dusk, *ja?* It is time to ready the longhouse if you do not want to sleep another night aboard the ship."

"*Ja!* And we want to take a nice bath, too! Get clean and sweet before bed!" agreed Thorvald.

"It will be a relief to get clean again," said Leif, shaking out his golden locks.

"Yes," said Ingmar, "we do get awfully ripe on board ship."

Reese gawked as Thorvald pulled out a bottle of lavender water. "I thought Vikings were supposed to be dirty and gross," he exclaimed without thinking.

"I beg your pardon!" said Leif. "I'll have you know we Vikings are very

careful about hygiene. No one likes a smelly fella."

"Indeed not," said Thorvald. He brought his face close to Reese's. "In fact, our young lad seems a bit fragrant himself!" He narrowed his eyes. "Did you brush your teeth this morning?"

"With *toothpaste?*" chimed in Ingmar.

"Enough! Get moving, crew!" ordered Leif. "Scrubbing bubbles time!"

As the Vikings grabbed soap, towels and other supplies, Reese thought fast. He'd been away from his class a while. Would they be out searching for him? What if the Vikings saw them? Would they do what Vikings did best — slaughter those who stood in their way? Reese couldn't let that happen.

"Wait!" he said. "If you go there now, um, trolls will get you! We Canadians use them as guards. Stay on board tonight where they cannot venture. In the morning, I'll arrange for you to challenge the Canadians. But I have to tell you, you won't beat them with your weapons. Battle-axes are very old-fashioned, you know. Haven't been used in these parts since 1106."

A grim whisper ran through the crew. He thought he heard Ingmar mutter something about "bath beads" and "no fair." Reese pressed on, hoping he wasn't about to be mashed into Norse meat.

"But Canadians love good competition," Reese continued. "Contests of strength and agility."

"Like who can jump the highest?" asked Thorvald.

"And run the fastest?" asked Ingmar.

"And eat the mostest," said Reese, nodding.

"That sounds good," Leif said. "We like contests like this."

"Then it's settled," said Reese. "I'll supply the competitors."

Leif and Reese spent most of the

night hammering out the events for the
match. Finally they agreed on five: the
long jump, high jump, battle-axe toss,
100-metre sprint and log lift. Now all
Reese had to do was tell his pals they'd
been entered into a track meet — and
that the future of Newfoundland
depended on them.

Chapter 4

Leif freed Reese just before dawn and sent him to arrange the challenge. His class was staying at a nearby campground.

Reese crawled into Randall's tent and found him snoring loudly. Reese clamped his hand over his friend's mouth. Randall woke with a start.

"Shh!" Reese said. "It's me. You'll

never guess what happened."

Randall pushed Reese's hand away and sat up.

"Let me guess. Kidnapped by Vikings?" he said dryly. "And now we have to, let's see . . . compete against them for your freedom?"

"Yeah — and for ownership of L'Anse aux Meadows."

"That's just great," said Randall. He rolled his eyes and threw himself back onto his sleeping bag. "Why do you have to keep stumbling across time travellers with *weapons?* Couldn't you trip over Laura Secord or something? *She'd* only have a cow and a box of chocolates."

"I think it might be because of this coin," Reese said, holding it up so Randall could see it. "I think it's got some magic to it. Its faces keep changing, see?"

Randall took the coin and rubbed his finger over the mysterious images.

"Freak-a-leaky …" Then he sighed. "What do we have to do this time?"

Reese replied, "Just a little track and field. No problemo, right?"

"Right. As long as the events don't include tossing battle-axes or other feats of Viking strength."

"Um . . ." Reese stammered.

"Thundering thunderbolts — you didn't!" exclaimed Randall, smacking his palm on his forehead.

"I had to compromise," Reese said sheepishly. "I got your best event in, though — the long jump. You're a sure winner at that."

"Who's supposed to hurl the battle-axe?" Randall asked.

"Well, you're an ace with a Frisbee . . ."

Randall smacked himself in the forehead again. "Odin, give me strength."

Chapter 5

A few hours later, Reese brought the Vikings to Norstead, a historical Viking village. It was the next stop on the Looney Bay tour. Actors dressed in costumes demonstrated what life had been like a thousand years ago. Reese hoped that the real Vikings would attract less attention here. He also hoped that their challenges might seem like part of the re-enactment.

"Okay, why don't you go over there," Reese pointed to a stone wall by a bog, "and get ready for the challenges? I'll go find my teammates."

"We will meet again soon, *ja*, McSkittles?" said Leif. "If you do not show up, then you forfeit this land and it is mine."

"We'll be here," said Reese. "But you can always change your mind and sail back to Greenland if you want . . ."

"We will never give up!" said Leif.

Reese went to see if his class had arrived yet. Several bright yellow buses were parked in the lot. He recognized Looney Bay's bus. Then he noticed a crest on one of the other buses and groaned. It was the crest of Trinity Bay Prep School — home of Looney Bay's arch-enemies, the Marauders!

Reese found his friends and shared the news.

"You mean we have to deal with Vikings *and* Marauders today?" asked Shannon in disbelief.

"Don't worry," said Reese. "It'll be fine."

"Yeah. Piece of cake," said Shannon, rolling her eyes.

Randall had already told the rest of the team about Reese's situation. The members of the track team huddled together to work out their strategy. They had barely finished their plan when they saw the Vikings crossing the bog. A few moments later they entered the village.

Leif hailed Reese. Then his eyes bulged. As he looked around the village, a broad grin creased his face. "Why, they live like kings here!" Leif exclaimed.

"Just like home, but better!" marvelled Thorvald.

"Yeah — there are Viking *girls!*" said Ingmar excitedly. "Pretty, well-scrubbed ones!"

"Actually they're Canadian girls," said Reese. "And, so what? They're just girls.

Let's get this match started.

"Thorvald, you're running the 100-metre against our fastest guy — Darren Willett. Are you both ready?"

Darren stepped forward. "Ready."

Thorvald stretched. "Ready."

"Then let's go," said Reese. "Laura's already marked off the course. So, on your marks . . ."

Thorvald and Darren squared off at the starting line, shooting evil glares at each other.

"Get set . . ." shouted Reese. "Go!"

Thorvald was bigger and stronger, but Darren was faster. Of course, it helped that Thorvald refused to drop his sword or shield.

Darren was about to take the lead when Thorvald stuck his sword out, forcing Darren to hurdle it until he fell. The All-Stars booed. Leif just laughed.

"There's more to winning than just speed. You also need cunning, *ja?*" he said.

Thorvald held his sword aloft at the

finish line. "I dare you to say I am not the winner!"

The Vikings took the lead, 1–0.

Next was the battle-axe toss. Randall struggled to lift the heavy weapon.

"Reese, couldn't you have made this a *coin* toss?" Randall moaned.

Ingmar stepped up to the mark. He began to spin around, gathering momentum. Then he let his battle-axe fly. It soared overhead, landing nearly a kilometre away in a clump of cloudberries.

The Vikings let out a collective groan.

"Oops," said Ingmar. "I'm feeling a little off today."

Randall dragged his battle-axe to the mark. He lifted it to his shoulder with enormous effort.

The All-Stars cheered for Randall, shouting, "You can do it!" Then they began a spirited count to urge him on.

On one, Randall began to spin. On

two, he kept spinning and spinning . . .
he couldn't stop!

On three, the battle-axe slipped from
his hands. It landed with a *clunk* not far
from his feet.

Randall fell dizzily to the ground.
His "throw" came in at a
whopping 14 centimetres.
The Vikings were ahead
2–0.

The third
event was the
high jump: Leif
versus Reese.

Reese went first. He
had his friends set the bar at his record
height. He took a deep breath and started running.

Reese felt the wind in his hair. The

ground beneath his feet was springy and soft. He felt like he was flying. He reached the bar and took it. He had easily matched his best jump ever!

Now it was Leif's turn. He, like Thorvald, refused to drop his sword or shield. But he was much taller than

Reese — Reese's bar was barely past Leif's waist.

Leif took the bar easily, hopping over it like a pebble on a sidewalk.

Shannon and Darren raised the bar two more centimetres. Reese's heart was pounding. He took another deep breath, then powered toward the bar. All of his concentration was focused on the jump. He leaped — he was clear!

Leif set off again for his jump. He ran smoothly and easily. It looked as if he would easily clear the bar, but at the last moment his sword, dangling at his side, knocked the stick off its frame. Reese had won!

It was 2–1 for the Vikings.

The next event was the long jump.

Randall was eager to make up for his

humiliation with the battle-axe.

Leif stepped up beside Randall. He carefully removed his sword, shield and helmet. "I will not miss this jump, too," he said through gritted teeth.

"I won't either," said Randall, warming up his legs by skipping in place.

When he was ready, he took off at a run. As Randall reached the mark, he

took one long stride and soared into the air. His legs and arms churned as if he were still running on land. His feet ploughed into the boggy ground, leaving a raw scar.

"Woo-hoo!" shouted the All-Stars. It was an awesome jump.

Then Leif began his run. He flew down the field and soared into the air.

He seemed to hang for an eternity. But when at last he returned to Earth, his heels landed short of Randall's mark.

The All-Stars had tied the match!

Now it was time for the final event: the log lift. A stack of logs was lying near the carpenter's shop. Leif plucked a hefty timber from the ground and said it was perfect.

Reese's heart sank as Laura Hook

studied the log. It was as big around as her waist and twice her height. Laura was a great athlete, but he doubted she could even budge the log, let alone lift it over her head.

Suddenly, the Vikings went berserk. They began shrieking their terrifying war cry. Confused, Reese and his friends ran for cover — also shrieking. But then they realized that the Vikings were running away from them. They were heading toward the shore, swords waving wildly in the air.

Four small canoes were entering the bay. Each held four or five warriors outfitted with spears and harpoons.

Skraelings!

Chapter 6

The Looney Bay All-Stars rushed to the beach. The Vikings were wading into the water, swords flashing in the sunlight. Arrows were flying at them from the Skraelings' boats. The All-Stars took a few steps back.

A tour guide with a name tag that read *My Viking Name is Mandy* was ushering a group of students onto the beach.

"Here you can see a battle between Vikings and natives from the Dorset culture. This native group disappeared completely about 1100 A.D. Cape Dorset is named for them. They weren't supposed to fight until 2 p.m., but I guess they rescheduled without telling me. Anyway, the Vikings called the natives 'Skraelings,' which in their language meant something like 'thin' or 'small.'"

"They look pretty big to me," said Randall. "Should we do something?"

"Like what?" said Reese. "Tell them to play nice?"

Someone shoved Reese from behind. "Yeah, you always wanna play nice, don't you, Reesy? You're just not tough enough to duke it out with the big kids."

It was Seamus, Reese's rival from the Trinity Bay Marauders! Flanking him were his two best buddies, Jack Patrick and Roman Quaig. They laughed like orangutans.

"Get lost, Seamus," said Reese.

"Make me," said Seamus, shoving Reese again.

"Whoa!" said Randall, stepping between them. "We're not barbarians. If we have a problem, let's settle it on the track."

"Oh sure," mocked Seamus. "We know you're good at running — away, that is!"

Jack and Roman sniggered. "Running away. That's a good one, Snodgrass."

"Oh really?" said Laura, stepping in. "I don't remember us running away when we trounced you at hockey."

The Looney Bay All-Stars stood together. "Or when we whupped you at lacrosse either," Randall said.

"Looks like the Trinity Babies have a selective memory," said Shannon, crossing her arms defiantly.

"Fine," sneered Seamus, "we challenge you! Four-man relay. Prepare to eat our dust."

"We'll see you in an hour," said Reese. "Behind the longhouse. Don't run late."

Seamus snorted once, then sauntered

off. Jack and Roman followed like two
little puppies.

A cheer rose from the crowd behind
the All-Stars. They turned to see the
Skraelings paddling off.

"The Vikings won!" said Randall.

"Well, let's hope that some of Leif's
luck rubs off on us," said Reese. "We're
going to need it."

Chapter 7

Reese congratulated Leif and explained the Marauders situation to him.

". . . and so we have this grudge match to run against the Marauders," Reese concluded.

"My men could just slaughter them."

"No, Leif. I've told you we don't settle scores like that in Canada any more. We do things the nice Canadian way."

"The Skraelings do not seem to know that," said Leif.

"That's because those Skraelings came from your time, Leif. They must have got here the same way you did. They're here for good."

"But if they are here for good," said Leif thoughtfully, "how will the peaceful, unsoiled villagers in this rich settlement defend themselves?"

"Good question, Leif," replied Reese.

Leif rose to his feet, slapped his thighs and called his men over. "My friends, we Vikings must stay and defend these villagers against the Skraelings. We cannot let the well-scrubbed girls get harpooned, *ja?*"

"*Ja!*" the Vikings cheered.

"So you don't want to challenge us

for the land anymore?" Reese asked.

"No, if we are to stay, we must try the new ways. We will help to protect the villagers from the old ways," said Leif.

"Okay," Reese said. "Then it's time to get ready for our challenge against the Marauders."

"May Odin give you swift feet," Leif said, slapping Reese on the back.

Chapter
8

An hour later Reese and the All-Stars
gathered behind the longhouse. Leif
and his men stood by, prepared to keep
the race fair and square.

Seamus appeared from around the
corner, with Jack, Roman and Dirty
Danny Fink.

"Let's do it," he said.

Leif handed sticks to Randall and to

Seamus. "The runners will go to the cloudberry bush and back. When you return, pass your baton to your teammate. The first team of four to complete the course wins.

"Now on your marks!" shouted Leif.

Randall and Seamus got into position.

"Get set!"

They bent down, knuckles in the dirt, their right legs stretched behind them.

"Go!"

Randall took the lead at the start, but Seamus gained and they were neck and neck. As they rounded the cloudberries, Randall got a better position.

He beat Seamus back

to the start and passed his baton to Laura.

Laura had a head start, but Jack put on the rockets and sped ahead. They were dead even when they passed their batons to Roman and Shannon.

Roman and Shannon zoomed down the course. As they came round the cloudberries, Shannon snagged her toe in a bramble. She lost her balance for a moment. Even though she caught herself, her slip let Roman take the lead. He handed his baton off to Danny while Shannon still had to cover the three last strides.

"Go! Go! Go!" urged Shannon as she pressed the baton into Reese's hand. "You can take him!"

Reese dug deep for an extra burst of

speed. He ran for all he was worth,
heart pounding, lungs straining. Inch by
inch, he closed the gap between himself and Danny.

He caught up to him at the cloudberries. The boys jostled each other as
they rounded the bend. Then Dirty
Danny pushed Reese down and took off.

"Hey!" shouted Ingmar, "That is not
playing the nice Canadian way, *ja?*"